D1312167

MR. CHEESEHEAD
Goes on a picnic...

by, T.J. Branson

copyright 2005 Vertigo Publishing

Copyright 2005
Vertigo Publishing
Now for the legal "Blah...Blah...Blah..." "The Adventures of Mr. Cheesehead..." and "Mr. Cheesehead goes on a picnic..." are the sole property of Vertigo Publishing. All rights reserved. No part of this publication may be reproduced in whole or in part, or stored in a retrieval system, or transmitted in any form or by any means, electronic, mechanical, photocopying, recording or otherwise, without written permission from the publisher. For information regarding permission write to:
Vertigo Publishing
PO Box 2683
Dearborn Michigan 48123

This book is
Dedicated to my wife Shelly,
I love you with all my heart...
Tim

International Standard Book Number:
0-9764463-3-2

First Edition / First Printing

Library of Congress Control Number:
2005925216

Published in the United States of America
by Vertigo Publishing

Printed in Korea

To find out more about this and other books in this series come visit us
@ www.vertigopublishing.com

Instructions for the listeners,

Every time the reader of this book says the name

"Mrs. Cheesehead"

you respond by saying

"Hi there" !

in your silly-ist, squeaky-ist, mousey-ist voice,
and every time the reader says either

"Playing"

or

"play"

you respond with

"Weeeee...Fun" !

Enjoy the story...

Here we go...

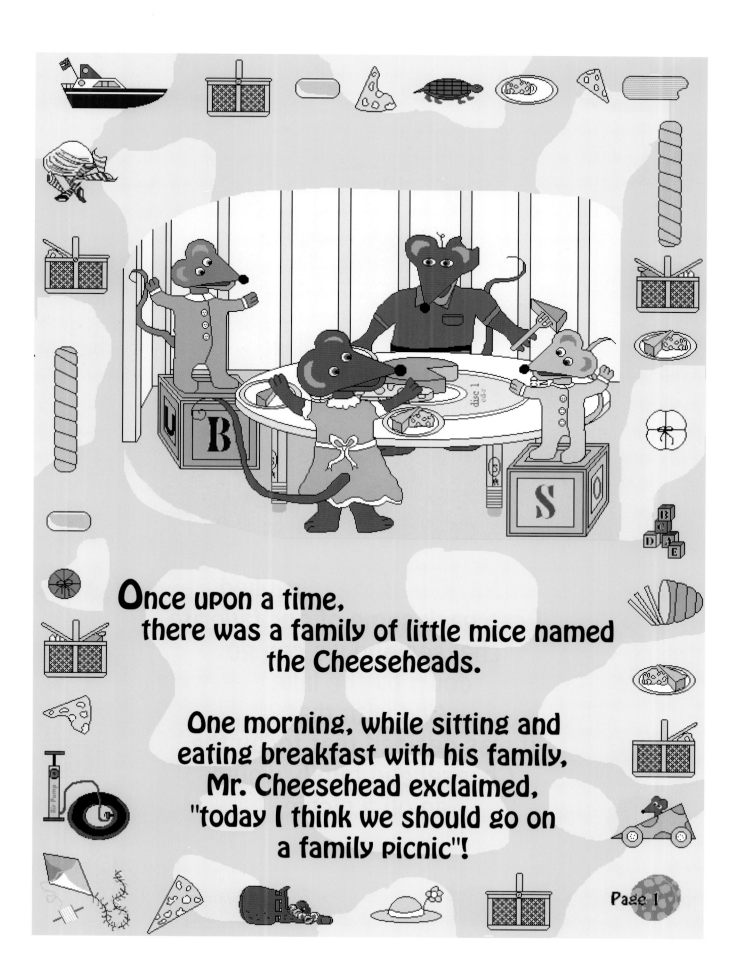

Once upon a time,
there was a family of little mice named
the Cheeseheads.

One morning, while sitting and
eating breakfast with his family,
Mr. Cheesehead exclaimed,
"today I think we should go on
a family picnic"!

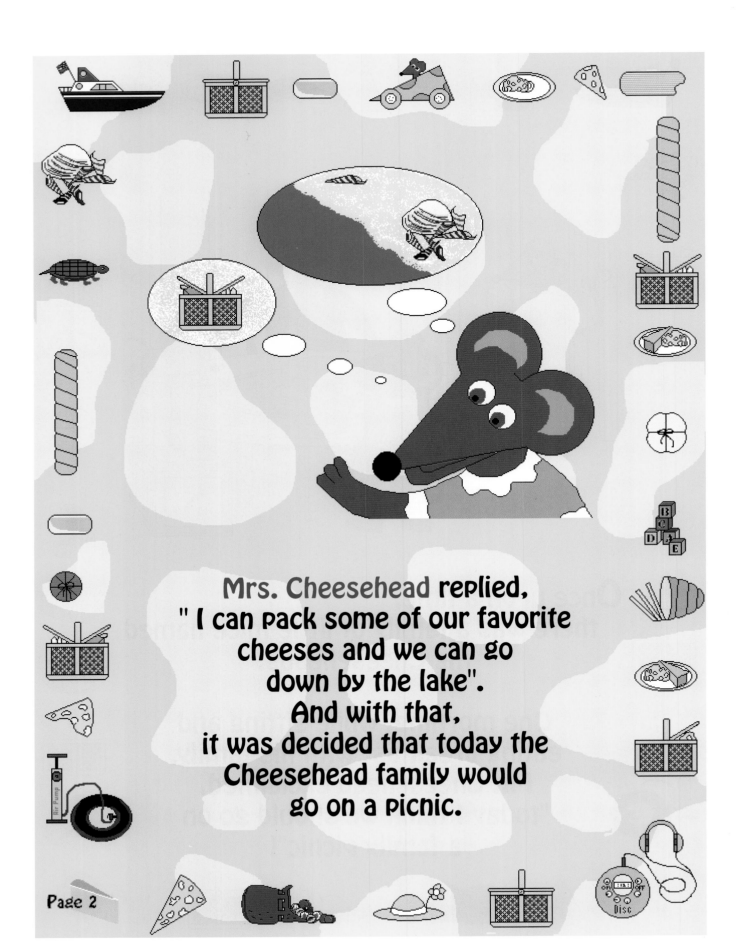

Mrs. Cheesehead replied,
" I can pack some of our favorite
cheeses and we can go
down by the lake".
And with that,
it was decided that today the
Cheesehead family would
go on a picnic.

While Mrs. Cheesehead was
gathering the food for their picnic,
Mr. Cheesehead and the children
collected everything else
they thought they might need.

Bubba packed...
his swimsuit, a blue towel, eleven
marbles, an old cork he shaped
into a boat, two of his favorite
comic books, six rubber bands,
his kite, a magnet, some building
blocks and most importantly
his pet turtle "Spike".

Smooches packed...
her favorite dolly "Pink Baby",
her blankie, her rock collection, two
different colored hats, a small
jewelry box, some dress up clothes,
her swimsuit, a nice pink towel, a
compact disc player, a couple of music
cd's and four purple balloons.

Mr. Cheesehead packed...
his swimsuit, a white towel, four
magazines, a radio, some batteries,
two pairs of shoes, a remote
controlled boat, **more batteries,** an
old inner tube, a blue air mattress, his
new mousetronics metal detector with
even more batteries
and a much needed air pump.

Mrs. Cheesehead... on the other hand
packed only her swimsuit, her towel,
a plaid wool blanket and their lunch.

When Mrs. Cheesehead noticed the collection of **stuff** that everyone else had packed, she politely asked "Must we take all of that for our picnic down by the lake"?

They all replied with a definite...

"Yes ma'am" !

So off to the lake they went.

When the Cheeseheads arrived
down by the lake, Mr. Cheesehead
and the children unloaded
all their gear while
Mrs. Cheesehead laid her soft wool
blanket out at the lakes edge and
prepared their lunch.

Then they all sat
around the blanket
and enjoyed the wonderful
lunch of different cheeses
that Mrs. Cheesehead
had prepared for them.

After the meal was over,
Mr. Cheesehead and the children
started to become very sleepy.

It seems that packing and
unpacking all of their stuff
turned out to be
very tiring work.

So,
the three of them took a little nap
under the afternoon shade
of a great old oak tree,

while...

Mrs. Cheesehead and Spike played with what everybody else had brought.

They spent the next two hours...

Playing

with Bubba's marbles
and...

BLOWING up Smooches' balloons

while **LISTENING** to music
and...

Help !

Reading **magazines,**
along with comic books
and...

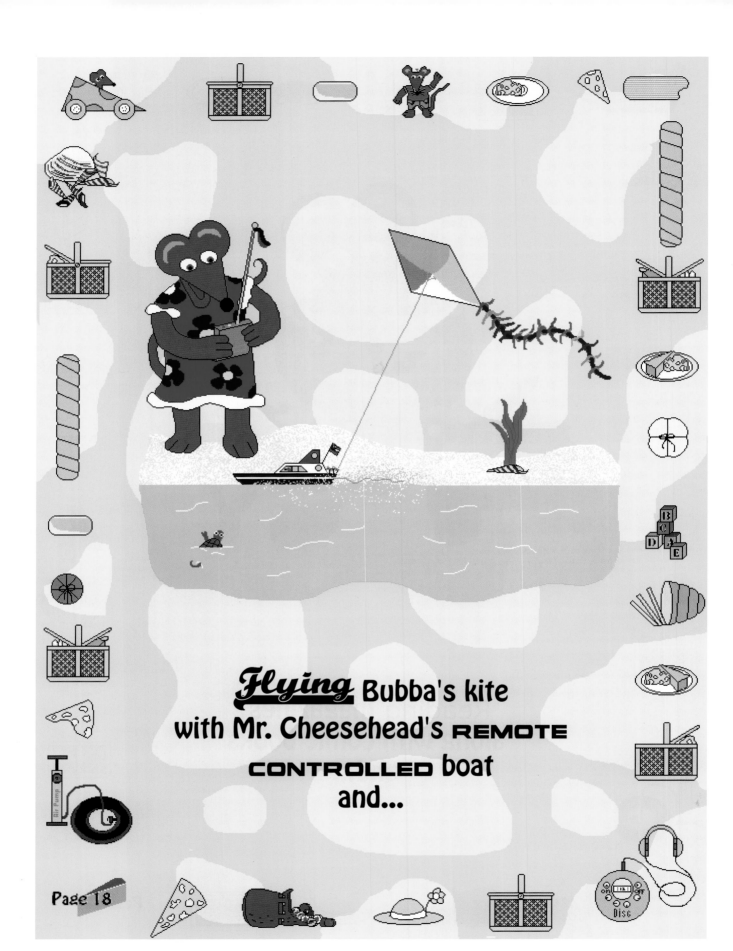

Flying Bubba's kite
with Mr. Cheesehead's REMOTE
CONTROLLED boat
and...

Playing dress-up with Smooches' dolly while ¡Umping up and down on the air mattress and...

searching
for buried treasure
with Mr. Cheesehead's new
metal detector
and...

Hi Spike!

Swimming in the lake

and

FLOATING on the inner tube!

Mrs. Cheesehead had just sat down,
to rest a little bit...

when Mr. Cheesehead and the
children awoke from their nap.

"Come on mom,
lets play with all our toys" !

The children exclaimed .

"No thank-you my dears, (yawn)
I think I'll just sit here, relax,
and enjoy the PEACE and Quiet".
replied Mrs. Cheesehead.

"Ok...
but you would have more fun playing,
than just sitting around all day".
Mr. Cheesehead added.

"Oh, I'm sure I would" !
Commented Mrs. Cheesehead,

thinking of her afternoon play-time,

"I'm sure I would" !!!

The End !
See you next time...

Every evening, just before bedtime, I read a book to my children, and after reading the same stories over and over again, they asked me to make them up their own story. So like some parents do, at one point in time, I started making up this silly story about a little mouse who lived over a cheese factory. When I mentioned the name "Mr.  Cheesehead", it made them giggle wildly, so together we embarked on the creation of " The Adventures of Mr. Cheesehead". After a couple of years of making up and telling of his escapades they still enjoy hearing these stories. I hope that your children giggle and enjoy them as much as I've enjoyed making them up.

Sincerely,

T.J.

Branson

DMC
Children's Hospital
of Michigan
DETROIT MEDICAL CENTER / WAYNE STATE UNIVERSITY

Since 1886, Children's Hospital of Michigan has been the only freestanding hospital in Michigan dedicated exclusively to caring for kids. Children's Hospital provides a wide variety of services for patients and their families in a comfortable environment. To learn more about Children's Hospital of Michigan or to find a doctor, call 313-745-KIDS or visit www.chmkids.org .

Vertigo publishing and T.J. Branson proudly support Children's Hospital of Michigan and in that spirit, $0.25 will be donated from every copy of this book sold.

Copyright © Vertigo Publishing 2005 USA